Brutal Tales

by

Ernesto Herrera

Translated by

Kathryn Phillips-Miles & Simon Deefholts

The Clapton Press

Brutal Tales by Ernesto Herrera

Original title: *Su Majestad el hambre (cuentos brutales)*
published by El Deber Cívico, 1910

Translated from the Spanish by
Kathryn Phillips-Miles & Simon Deefholts

Cover design and illustrations by Ivana Nohel

First published 2022 by:
The Clapton Press Limited
38 Thistlewaite Road, London E5

ISBN: 978-1-913693-12-1

*This work has been published within the framework of the
IDA Translation Support Program*

Ministry
**of Education
and Culture**
URUGUAY

National Directorate
of Culture

Uruguay *XXI*
INVESTMENT, EXPORT AND COUNTRY
BRAND PROMOTION AGENCY

Contents

A Brief Note on the Author

Ernesto Herrera was born in Montevideo in 1889 and died in 1917, a month short of his twenty-eighth birthday. He first travelled to Europe in 1909 via Buenos Aires, where he was thrown off a ship as a stowaway, eventually making his way to Lisbon, and onward to Madrid. In Barcelona he was arrested and locked up in the Modelo Prison, for reasons not documented, although in one of his short stories, *The Quagmire*, allegedly written in the prison itself, the protagonist had been incarcerated for insulting the monarchy. He was deported back to South America the same year. Before returning to Montevideo he spent some time in Brazil, writing for two local anarchist newpapers.

On his return to Uruguay, Herrera produced articles under various pen-names as well as a series of "brutal tales" for a local newspaper, *El Deber Cívico*. Fifteen of these were reproduced in a short anthology in 1910, under the title *Su Majestad el Hambre: Cuentos Brutales*, which are now published here in English for the first time, together with a sixteenth story from the same period, *Sucesión*. As the title of the collection suggests, the stories are not subtle, forcefully conveying the author's anger at the injustice and brutality that he perceived in contemporary Uruguayan society.

In subsequent years Herrera focussed on the stage, producing nine plays, the last of which was unfinished. His first play was perhaps the most famous. *El león ciego (The Blind Lion)*, produced in the Teatro Cibilis in Montevideo in 1911, was based on his experiences during the political violence between "Blancos" (members of the right-wing National Party) and "Colorados" (members of the ruling Colorado party), which he had witnessed as a journalist the previous year. 1911 also saw the birth of his son, Barrett. The following year he made another journey to Europe, spending the next 18 months in Paris and Madrid. He returned to Montevideo in June 1914, due to ill-health. While he was away, Ofilia Silva, Barrett's mother, had committed suicide.

Herrera died after a short spell in hospital, from a throat infection, in February 1917.

Prologue

Your Majesty, Hunger, Empress of the world, all-powerful lady who rules over the towering peaks and the cavernous depths, this book is dedicated to you. Because you inspired it, you made me experience it, because everything contained within it belongs to you.

You, ma'am, have been my inseparable companion throughout all my anguish, throughout my intense and beautiful life. When you lay down beside me, on those unforgettable nights (so long and so cold); when in the frenzy of orgasms you dug your sharp feline claws into my flesh; when you told me about your many lovers and you made me share all your voluptuous experiences; when we looked at the world through your bloodshot eyes, like two red windows; when we wandered across your dominions; when we flew over your attic rooms in the Latin Quarter of Montmartre and then descended into the filthy mire of all your taverns, all your brothels and all your prisons, that's when I began to understand you and that's when I learned how to love you.

And it was your love, your cruel, overwhelming love, that taught me to grit my teeth and smile indulgently. So, this book is for you. This book, the good and the bad, the simple and the complicated, the amorous and the perverse; because you inspired it, because everything contained within it belongs to you.

Preface

Rodó said recently that 'in our day and age, even those of us who are not socialists, or anarchists, or anything of the kind, either in our actions or our beliefs, have a predisposition (of which we are aware to a greater or lesser extent) for protest, discontent, and 'inadaptability' in the face of so much brutal injustice, so many hypocritical lies, so much entrenched and hateful vulgarity, that are all woven into the fabric of the social order that has been passed down to the twentieth century, a century that has dawned with the emergence of a bourgeoisie and a utilitarian democracy.'

This feeling of 'inadaptability' or non-acceptance is inseparable from life. The assumption, implicit in the former idea of evolution, that 'life adapts to its surroundings' is disappearing from the science of biology. It may perhaps be relevant to the lower organisms, forever condemned to automatism and then to a slow final extinction, but for superior organisms (such as mammals and birds) with their high degree of versatility, the more precise formula is that life, far from adapting, rebels against its physical environment, and forces the environment to adapt. This is more than proven by the classic example that the blood temperature of modern vertebrates is much higher than the average temperature of air and water. Man has also succeeded in warming the air that surrounds him, and in making less propitious climates habitable. To adapt to the present is to renounce the future. And if we consider the social environment, we understand that the course of progress has been analogous, and that it is the extraordinary ability that certain individuals possessed to not adapt to their environment and to hold out against it, countering an external reality with a prophetic, internal reality, that has made the world go round. All the utopian ideals: the abolition of slavery and serfdom, the suppression of ecclesiastical authority, monarchical and aristocratic privileges, have taken hold successively, after originally being the inspired vision of the great innovators, and no educated thinker is unaware today that the only true utopia is a conservative utopia.

Ernesto Herrera is a typical 'non-adapter'. The speed and volume of communication and advertising, as well as democratic practices, place us in daily contact with all the evils and horrors from across the globe. On the other hand, as moral standards are raised and society cleans up its act, the desire for justice becomes more intransigent, more exasperating, more painful. The more we try to make ourselves perfect, the more our perception of the enormous amount of work that remains to be done becomes cruelly apparent. In the case of Ernesto Herrera, add to these generalities the fact that he has experienced poverty, been a victim of persecution and has suffered from neglect and anguish, and we can understand why such blood-curling sentences sprout from the pen of this still naïve, embittered

16

adolescent. Herrera belongs to the noble caste of the ill at ease. Sacred uneasiness, mother of all creation! You who are contented should understand that your happiness is nothing more than the part of you that is dead inside. Contented people—dead people shunted from here to there by the living—should understand that the only thing that works is uneasiness. May fate grant Ernesto Herrera the energy required to continue working for a long time yet and to hold aloft the shadowy trophies of anguish!

Rafael Barrett, San Bernadino (Paraguay), August 1910.

Parallel Lives

He was there night after night, halfway down the dark alleyway, seemingly deep in thought, with his head bowed and his tail between his legs, his bones barely covered by a pathetic, ragged, mangy coat, whining grumpily as hunger led him from one bin to another, scratching, sniffing and searching in vain. He was a genuine street dog, a miserable cur, stoned by the children and beaten by the grown-ups, humiliated at every turn. No collar, no kennel, no tag, no beggar to accompany, no ageing spinster to sweeten his wretched life with treats.

Damned inequality! I would see him wandering around, hungry; I would see him growling at the spoilt lapdogs of the privileged classes as they trotted past, I would see him glare at them contemptuously, as if spitting a vile insult in their faces, labelling them as miserable slaves.

He was my friend, why should I hide it? He was my friend.

When he heard my footsteps in the middle of the night, when he saw me heading towards the dark alleyway, he would always come and greet me. He would come and greet me with dignity, as an equal, without any servile tail wagging, or jumping, or growling, and we would negotiate the gloomy alleyway together.

We understood each other. He was the only dog who didn't bark at me aggressively whenever he saw my dirty, ragged figure approach; I was the only man who didn't turn my head away in disgust or raise my stick menacingly whenever I saw him.

The two of us both felt a deep-seated contempt towards our own species, the same hatred. We undoubtedly shared the same story, so the dog took pity on me when he saw I was dirty and ragged, and I admired that pathetic, mangy skeleton of a dog, the only noble, dignified rebel in a whole race of slaves.

* * *

You can guess the ending. All his suffering, all his hatred, all his contempt exploded one day: the dog caught rabies. He ran through the streets in a fury, biting whoever he met and spreading the virus vengefully; he was finished off with a bullet, just as he was enjoying his triumph, after making his torturers tremble.

As for me, you know my story. All my hatred and all my contempt exploded too. When the bomb went off and I saw a hundred of my torturers fall all around me, covered in blood and shredded to pieces, I too felt avenged. Just like the dog, I feel noble; just like the dog I have had my vengeance. So what, then, if tomorrow my life will end in the same way as the dog's?

* * *

That was what the wretched man told me. That was what the evil terrorist, condemned by others to pay for his crime on the scaffold, told me. That was what he told me, with the simple eloquence of the truth, with the steady voice of conviction.

I watched him walk calmly to his death and then I contemplated his corpse hanging on the end of a rope, swinging in the air. Then I remembered the dog. I thought about how justified his vengeance was, and I thought about how much their lives had in common, and I almost envied them both. I felt a sense of solidarity with those rebels, that pair of hydrophobics, and I turned round to have one last look at my friend. His lifeless body was still swaying there, like the pendulum of an enormous clock that eventually, come what may, will mark the hour.

The Pie

'A story from my bohemian days?' asked X, the famous poet. 'Happy days! Who could recall them without their heart brimming over with all those memories, bitter or sweet, of times that we shall never see again, much to our chagrin?' And he rested his head between his hands, still smiling wistfully. Then he continued:

'At the time I was barely more than a boy. I'd left home in search of new horizons. I'd landed in the capital with nothing more than a few coins in my pocket, love in my heart and a whole host of ideas in my starry-eyed head. The capital, where everyone is rich and dies of hunger. And that was all.

Was I already a poet, a real poet? I'd like to think I was, and even more so than now, and yet . . .

My first few months in the capital were an interminable series of endless days going without food, freezing with cold, beset with disappointment . . . above all, disappointment!

In my childish naivety I had thought that I would dazzle everyone with the first lines I wrote. I dreamt of publishers fighting over my books, enthusiastic readers praising my work and crowning me with laurels; in other words, I dreamt of glory.

The day it happened was the third day I had gone without any food at all. I had left my attic room, crazed with hunger and chilled to the bone, and strode into the street like a lunatic, carrying the manuscript for my first book under my arm. Was I looking for a scrap to eat or was I looking for a publisher? Even I didn't know.

I wandered aimlessly for several hours, constantly bumping into the passers-by thronging the streets. It was around seven in the evening, on a winter's night. It was raining, freezing cold, with no moon or stars in the sky. There were people everywhere, all in a hurry: workers, seamstresses; the world of work was like a monster that had just disgorged its lunch!

Everyone was in a hurry, everyone was cold and hungry, but it was not a gnawing hunger, it was not all-consuming. It was a simple question of appetite, there to be immediately assuaged with a steaming plate of soup on a snowy white tablecloth. My hunger was greater than that and would endure for longer. I didn't have a family waiting for me impatiently at home; no one would serve me in a restaurant. And I was hungry! That was when I thought of my family, my parents, my childhood home and the simple meals we ate by the warm fire. Oh! If only I could be like everyone else. I wept. However, regretting my moment of weakness I straightened my back once more, trying in vain to escape from my sorrows. It was the first time that I had felt the weight of my talent on my shoulders.

I only remember the most climactic moments from the events of that day; all I know is that I wandered for hours and hours along the damp streets, until at last I came to a halt in front of a shop window, bedazzled. The shop was a *rotisserie*. In the centre of their window display, just to tease me, was a splendid turkey pie, garnished with lettuce leaves and aspic. Such cruel irony! I didn't know whether to yawn or retch as I stared through the thick pane of glass! Written in black letters on a little white card placed next to the pie was the price: one-fifty. One-fifty! Did such a fabled amount really exist?

I walked off without looking back, fleeing from the temptation to commit a smash and grab. I carried on for a hundred yards, sighed, and came to a halt once more. I had just seen a sign above a bookshop door that read: 'Publisher'.

I went in and asked for the owner, and after waiting for an interminable length of time, I was led to a small room that served as an office. Sitting there was the Messiah, God himself, talking to a man with chubby cheeks, who looked like a retired shopkeeper.

I don't remember what I told them. I know that I strung together a series of incoherent words, that I spoke about publication . . . success . . . glory. What can I say? The vision of that cursed pie prevented me from being concise.

The publisher listened, observing me with pity; the chubby-cheeked man smiled with contempt. Talk about a misspent youth . . . writing poetry! As if poetry would earn enough to pay for a wretched pie!

I stifled their protests and read my first poems out loud, whether they liked it or not. At the end of each page, I glanced up hopefully at the publisher. And each time the wretch would shake his head. Finally, I reached the passage in my first poem which spoke about enchanted fountains. It was so beautiful and I read it so enthusiastically. But nothing.

"They're not bad," the wretched publisher said, interrupting me, "but it's impossible."

I looked at the chubby-cheeked man as if begging for assistance. I noticed that he looked serious and thoughtful, as if reflecting on some very tricky business deal. Then he asked me, "How much do you want for those manuscripts, young man?"

"One-fifty," I replied hopefully.

And the man held out his hand.

"I'll take them."

"What are you going to do with them?" I asked the man, who still looked a little distracted.

"Nothing, it's just that passage about the fountains . . ."

"That's the best bit of poetry I've ever written," I responded proudly, but the man shook his head and smiled contemptuously.

"Well, it's not exactly that," he replied. "It's just, if we make some changes to the last two lines, they'll make a perfect advertisement for my mineral water."

And he held out the two coins, magnanimously.

I don't know what came over me; my eyes glazed over and I wanted to toss the coins back in his face, leap at his throat and throttle him, but suddenly the image of that pie took hold of me. I reached out for the coins like an automaton and, without even saying goodnight, I ran off towards the *rotisserie*.'

An Infanticide

'Any mother who kills her own child is an animal,' said Z, the young lawyer, dogmatically, in a sententious tone of voice that wise men use occasionally and fools use invariably. Everyone agreed.

'Worse than an animal,' added the Marchioness of R, a voluptuous blonde who had been married for three years and boasted of using the best method to avoid bearing children, which only disfigures one's face and destroys a slim figure, 'because animals love their offspring, and will even lay down their lives for them.'

'May I join the discussion?'

Everyone turned towards the corner the voice had come from. Sitting comfortably in an armchair, an elderly man was observing the gathering, his blue eyes glinting in friendly irony.

'By all means. The floor is yours.'

'Do you have a story for us, Señor Guerin?' asked the hostess, while the other members of the group formed a circle around the elderly man.

'A simple case, madam, a simple case.'

'Ah, when it comes to wild animals, they're ten to the dozen!' the young lawyer chipped in.

'Oh no, my friend, this is not a case of blind instinct. The court reports are full of cases of truly ferocious infanticides, as you say, as a result of hunger and family pressures, because extramarital motherhood is always considered a dishonour, a monstrous crime, but my story is not about one of those. It's about a case of infanticide committed by someone fully aware of what they were doing, a completely humanitarian act.'

There was a rumble of disapproval, but the elderly man continued unabashed.

'It was quite a few years ago. I was fairly young at the time. I'd only been practising a short while and I'd achieved one of my most cherished dreams. I had just been appointed as a judge in the city of R. As I said, I was fairly young at the time and I was full of optimism about everything to do with my profession. Ever since I was a child, reading novels, I had built up a stereotype of the ideal judge, an authentic Cimourdain in robes, an implacable administrator of the law, unwaveringly virtuous, terribly inflexible.'

'So back in those days you were not as sceptical as you are now?'

'No, madam, no. My scepticism came later. At that time, I was a true optimist. I believed in the law, I believed in mankind, I believed in God, in a God who was a judge, like me and who, like me, applied justice efficiently and in a humanitarian way. That's why I was so enthusiastic about my role as a judge. I was so naïve!'

'But Señor Guerin! In that case you don't believe . . .'

'I don't believe in the law, no, madam. And I began not to believe in it precisely when the event that I want to tell you

30

about occurred.'

'All right. Let's hear your story.'

'Excellent. Listen to this. I was a judge, and one day I happened to sit in a trial which dashed all my long-held convictions to the ground. The case involved a young woman, a newly-wed accused by her own husband of killing a child conceived from their marriage. During the trial, she didn't deny the crime. The facts were that she had given birth to a baby boy some two months previously and had smothered him with the bedclothes. And so in full awareness of her actions, in cold blood, that mother had killed her own child.'

'What a woman!' the young lawyer shouted.

'How very brave!' the marchioness commented. 'And that's what you call a humanitarian infanticide?'

The narrator smiled again and carried on, calm and composed.

'As I told you, she didn't deny the crime, but she did explain it. She had been married for 'family expediency' to a man who was sick, a genuine case of hereditary degeneration. Her husband was an atavistic drunkard, a libertine, a person who was morally and physiologically wasted. Anticipating future developments and all the time obsessed with the idea of moral responsibility, she had tried every means of avoiding pregnancy, but nature is almost always terribly cruel in such cases and one day the poor woman felt, stirring inside her, an innocent wretch, a future degenerate, damned before he was born.

That was when she formed a resolute plan to use every possible means to prevent it from happening. She tried everything, she exhausted every procedure and the child continued to develop, turning in her womb, like a curse that would fatefully come to pass.

By the time she gave birth, everything was already determined. One day she picked up the child, gave him lots of kisses and then smothered him. In cold blood, as a humanitarian act. There was no possible doubt. Humanity might applaud but the law must punish and a judge is obliged to obey the law. So I sent that woman to jail. What do you say to that?'

'What nonsense,' the marchioness exclaimed. 'That woman was a fool. I mean, to do such a thing, when there was so much more she could have done! In *The Intruder*, by D'Anunzio . . .'

'That's not the point,' the young lawyer interrupted, gravely. 'Let's look at it from a legal perspective. Did that woman have the right to kill her child?'

'That's not the point, either,' the elderly man replied. 'Let's look at it from a human perspective. Did that mother have the right to let him live?'

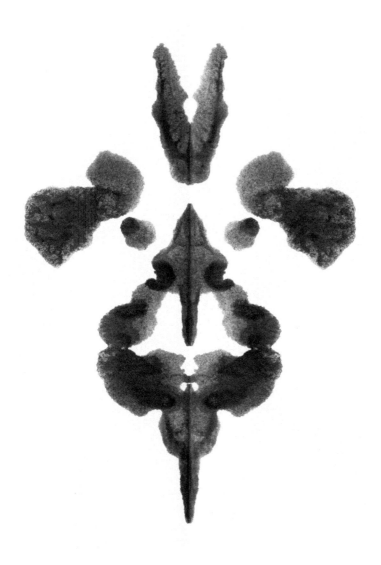

33

The Condemned Man

'Our Father, who art in Heaven . . .'

'Pray, my son, pray, because God is infinitely good and infinitely just. Pray, my son.'

'Our Father, who art in Heaven . . .'

And you could hear him whispering the prayers, one after another, always rounded off with an 'Amen' from the good priest, always preceded by the sobs of the wretched penitent. Afterwards, it all fell silent. There, in an adjacent room, a fateful clock counted each second that passed with a menacing tone. Then, more sobs and once again the monotonous whispering:

'Our Father, who art in Heaven . . .'

The chapel is very depressing. A small, improvised altar on a pine table covered with a black cloth with silver flecks. Four candles that bathe the room with their flickering, blood-red light, weeping tears of wax; a statue of Christ with a yellowing face, his head resting on his chest, eyes raised to heaven, half ironic and half asleep. Two men seated at the end of the table; one of them elderly, the other adolescent; the priest and the condemned man; the confessor and the penitent. Nothing more.

* * *

The poor wretch was about to die but was still full of life. He was twenty-two years old with a big heart, good health and he'd had everything to look forward to. He'd been deeply in love with a beautiful woman. He'd had a peaceful home and an angelic little boy. Now all he had left was his life, and tomorrow they would strip him of the last of his possessions.

How had all this happened? How could those events have occurred? Memories swirled around the poor wretch's head. Shadows, shadows and nothing but shadows. What became of all that happiness?

And he clenched his fists and bit his lips and tasted his own blood. Blood! Blood of men, blood of beasts. He felt so thirsty!

How stupid he'd been! He'd been a good man for so many years! Today he might have been able to put up a defence; today maybe they wouldn't have taken from him everything they had taken. But back then, he'd been too good and that was why they had stripped him of everything.

He'd had a friend, he'd had a wife, he'd had a son, he'd had a home and he'd been happy. And then . . .

His friend had stolen his wife; his wife had stolen his friend; death had carried away his son, and along with all that, his home and his happiness and his hopes and everything good had gone up in smoke too. They'd broken his heart and now they complained that he was evil.

* * *

36

Daybreak. The cocks screech their first 'good mornings' and the guard dogs bark their final warnings. The clock chimes five. Then a key turns in a lock and a door opens. They're the last in a line of thieves and they're coming for the only thing he has left. The miserable wretch watches them approach and he stands between them silently, resignedly. He thinks of his wife, he thinks of his son, he thinks of his friend, he thinks of his fellow men.

The priest is standing next to him and whispers final words of comfort in his ear; he speaks of God's infinite mercy . . .

38

A Story for Mimí

Shall I tell you a story, Mimí? A simple story, a sad story, a story that portrays our lives and makes us think? All right then, I'll tell you a story.

Once upon a time there were two dark eyes; two eyes set in the heavenly marble of a doll's little face, that recounted her dreams miraculously. They had been with her as she talked to herself in the mirror, her confidante around the clock. Her eyes were accompanied by a tiny little nose and a bright red mouth that were both terribly proud of being so delightfully close to her eyes.

When I saw them for the first time, when the dark flames of those pupils burned into me for the first time, a mysterious spell took hold of me; the night overcame my heart and my dreams wandered through my soul one after the other in a long procession that was bluer than blue.

What do you think, Mimí? Was the woman who owned those eyes some beautiful fairy-tale princess? No. The owner of those eyes was someone much greater, infinitely more human than that; the owner of those eyes was a *cocotte* and she shared the same name as you. Doesn't that make you feel uncomfortable? Her name was Mimí.

I met her one night, she made love to me for an hour and I never saw her again. It was a wonderful night, a tropical night, full of light and fire, like the two enormous nights in her eyes. I was wandering around as usual, staring up at the stars, at those white slaves of the celestial harem when, as I crossed a side road as sad and lonely as my soul, I felt an arm linking with mine and I heard a sweet little voice telling me ever so softly, almost directly in my ear, 'Fancy going for a stroll together?'

I looked away from the sky in order to see who had spoken to me and I could barely notice the difference. Instead of the silvery stars shining brightly in my imagination, there before my eyes I could see her pupils, like two black stars. I wrapped my arm tight around her waist and stole a kiss, and we strolled along like this for quite some time, just as the two of us are doing now, the magical moonlight being sublimely delighted (as it is right now, too) to act as our priest.

She told me her life story, just like that, without me asking, without any introductions, like a soul that has long felt the need to confide in another like hers. She was a *cocotte*. She gave herself gloriously to her lovers by the hour, to avoid selling herself miserably her whole life long. She had loved many times, always whole-heartedly, but never for more than one season. Many men had been close to her and worshipped at her feet; she had loved them all deeply and they had all madly assumed that she would love them for ever.

'The fools!' she added, with an expression of delightful scorn. 'Couldn't they understand that the boredom would have killed me?'

In short, we were very much in love, Mimí; every bit as

much (don't get tetchy) as we two love each other now. And we spent a whole summer full of happiness, as if it would never end. Then, when the grey weather arrived and the first dry yellow leaves began to fall, I lost her. Into the arms of death? No. Into the arms of another lover who came between us, offering her new caresses and new embraces.

One day, when I came back to my attic room, I found on my desk a perfumed letter, in which the words 'luv' and 'forget abowt me' told me all I needed to know about Mimí's absence. The present had become the past, happiness had become a memory, an illusion that was never more than an illusion. That was what made me love her even more and what made our love sublime.

Do you understand?

My Neighbour, Don Alejo

If someone had knocked on my door just a few days ago and told me that Satan himself had come in person for my neighbour, Don Alejo's soul, I would have rushed downstairs without hesitating (even though I'm not a courageous man), determined to challenge the horned angel's claim to what I considered as rightfully belonging to the Lord.

'A man more saintly than Don Alejo,' I used to say enthusiastically, 'would have to be born of the Virgin, God willing, because an ordinary woman could not give birth to a man of his calibre!'

And such was my enthusiasm and such my admiration for the saintliness of my neighbour that, leaning on the balcony that overlooked his garden, I would spend entire mornings watching him scuttle to and fro between the bird cages and kennels. It seemed that the only creatures my excellent neighbour really loved were his pets, and how he loved them! His garden was filled to the brim with animals of every shape and size! It was nothing less than a Noah's Ark.

Dogs, cats, wolves, doves, monkeys . . . in short, every type of beast, which my neighbour had made his family and in which he would invest the huge amount of tenderness and affection held in his heart. That man was so patient! You should have seen him in the mornings, in his shirt sleeves, rushing from one bird cage to the next, bringing lettuce and salad leaves and hard boiled eggs one minute and olive oil the next, to add to the bird seed. You should have seen him, carefully checking his dogs' kennels, the monkeys' and the parrots' cages, leaving a treat in each one, offered tenderly to his fortunate guests, who greeted him turning pirouettes in a clear demonstration of affection and gratitude. All in all, Don Alejo was a saint.

He was fifty years of age, wealthy, with no family and no friends (details which earned my childish admiration). He led a simple life, dedicated exclusively to the care of his menagerie. He treated them all as equals. As if they were his children!

'What a kind soul!' I would say to myself from my vantage point. 'What a kind soul!' And I spent hours and hours waiting anxiously for the opportunity to engage with him, in a brief dialogue on whatsoever subject, so that I could call this most saintly of men my friend.

That is why, when my valet told me yesterday that something 'really serious' was going on in my saintly neighbour's garden, I leapt out of bed without even bothering to look for my trousers and shot over to my 'observatory', desperate to find out what was happening to the animals' saintly protector, the idol I adored.

There was a great hullabaloo. Twenty or so onlookers had invaded the garden, much to the annoyance of a similar number of civil guards, and they were all gathered round in a circle. In the centre, Don Alejo was furiously clutching a small boy of around six years old by the wrist. The boy was crying without let up, while a police inspector made inquiries to ascertain exactly what had happened.

'He broke into my garden!' the saintly Don Alejo screamed, furiously. 'And he spent the night in Top's kennel! The poor little dog has been howling since daybreak, and rightly so! He's almost frozen to death!'

And as Don Alejo passed the young miscreant over to the custody of the police inspector with one hand, with the other he tenderly stroked the shiny coat of a handsome greyhound, who was rubbing against his legs affectionately.

'Outrageous! Making him spend a whole night like that!'

A Pessimistic Interlude

One stretch of coastline which can be really lovely is Punta Carretas (if I were a modernist, I'd have said Biarritz). Lying face down between some rocks, facing the sea, a man is humming a *canzonetta*. He looks like a tramp, with a grubby, tattered hat and his multicoloured clothes are dishevelled and covered in dust.

A new character arrives. He is young and elegantly dressed, and his wide-brimmed hat betrays his profession. (Don't panic! I won't make him recite!)

The young man walks down towards the sea shore, watching the waves ebbing and flowing for a few moments, then he turns round and catches sight of the tramp who has now has stopped singing.

* * *

Young man (surprised): 'Anyone would think you were dead.'

Tramp (without looking up): 'You're good at reading people's faces. I am a dead man, nothing more, nothing less.'

Young man: 'So, what are you doing over there?'

Tramp: 'I'm thinking. It's the ultimate resort for those of us who can't think.'

Young man: 'Ah! I see. You sound like a philosopher, but

you're a tramp.'

Tramp: 'I was right when I said that you could read people's faces!'

Young man: 'You're interesting. Do you smoke?' (He offers him a cigarette).

Tramp (half sitting up): 'What? Do these things still exist? I thought there was nothing left but dog-ends.' (He takes a cigarette and takes a light from the young man).

Young man: 'What's your name?'

Tramp (taken by surprise): 'Are you a policeman?'

Young man: 'No, why do you ask?'

Tramp (reflective): 'It's strange. Only the police have ever asked me that question. What's my name? If I'd known who my father was I could have asked him, but my mother didn't know, either.'

Young man: 'Ah, you have a mother?'

Tramp: 'Yes . . . I mean, no. I don't have a mother and she doesn't have a son. We're two quite separate entities.'

Young man (pausing to think for a moment): 'Do you like the sea?'

Tramp: 'It has its drawbacks. These sea breezes give you an incredible appetite.'

Young man: 'Yes, but what about the waves, the sound.'

Tramp: 'I'd like them better if they didn't remind me so much of people and the general population.'

Young man: 'People and the general population?'

Tramp: 'Yes, haven't you ever noticed? Look, last night the

sky suddenly clouded over, the sea started to become rough and roar, as if it wanted to rebel against the coast that was holding it back, and flood everything. When it all comes down to it, the sea was right. It has plenty of water so why shouldn't it go where it pleases? There was a sound of thunder, roaring like a demagogue. The waves reared up as high as a mountain, terrifying, rabid and topped with foam, then flung themselves against the coast like a great avalanche crashing down.'

Young man: 'What happened next?'

Tramp: 'Next, they dissolved into foam. The thunder interrupted their debate and then everything was the same as it had been before. And today, there it is, gently lapping against the sand. Like the general population!'

Young man: 'You know, you've got quite a gift.'

Tramp: 'That's saying something! If I were an ordinary brute, I wouldn't be lying here dead, I'd be a skilful politician, I'd know how to add and subtract, multiply and divide, and I'd have some kind of profession: a respectable banker, managing director of a business enterprise, a shameless moneygrubber, a grandee, a wise man . . .'

Young man: 'Why don't you stand on your own two feet and fight?'

Tramp: 'Fight? Who with? What for? They'd all be against me. They'd flatter me to my face and slander me behind my back. I'd be a laughing stock and they'd end up despising me.'

Young man: 'Yes, but . . .'

Tramp: 'You're right. They'd put up a statue of me after I

died.'

Young man: 'Why don't you kill yourself, then.'

Tramp: 'It's pointless. I did that already. I'm dead.'

Young man: 'Yes, but you're not a corpse.'

Tramp: 'It makes no difference. I'm a dead man, with the advantage that I don't rot. I don't want to be altruistic even to the worms. Now do you understand why I don't stand up?'

Young man: 'You're not being fair. People . . .'

Tramp: 'Dirty pig! Get out of here with that filth!'

Young man: 'I'm not convinced. Man has a duty to fight, to make his mark. Life demands it and life itself rewards it. Look at how beautiful nature is over there; so fertile, so full of light? Look at those huge fields, and the sterile deserts like sexual virgins waiting to match up their strength with their vitality in order to explode into life? It's all beautiful, sweet and grandiose: the sky above, all blue or all encrusted with stars; the sea down below, the fertile fields, the shady forest and the tall and graceful mountains . . . You don't know the beauty of life!'

Tramp: 'You've just had a decent meal, haven't you?'

Young man: 'How did you know that?'

Tramp: 'Because you sound as if you have indigestion.'

Young man: 'Maybe so, but my words come from the soul, not the stomach. That's because I'm happy, can't you understand?'

Tramp: 'So I see, but I don't envy you. If I'd been happy in the past, I'd be having a rough time now, my friend. And anyway, I don't think anyone has any reason to be happy.'

Young man: 'That's because you don't know . . .'

Tramp: 'Of course I know. Look: you're one of many, a dreamer, nothing more or less than a dreamer. You think you're happy and brimming over with joy. You needed to tell someone and since you know what men are like you came down here to confide in the sea. You thought you could tell it all to the waves, but you found me. I told you I was dead and now you can't wait to shower me with your secrets, like a man with a blunderbuss. But I'll save you the trouble. I know all about it. Let's cut to the chase: why are you so happy? Maybe you're in love?'

Young man: 'But . . .'

Tramp: 'Yes, yes. You saw her last week or yesterday or today, at a dance, or maybe in a garden, yes, it must have been in a garden. She's as pretty as an angel, more beautiful than the dawn, her skin is as white as the snow on the mountain peaks and her voice is as sweet and harmonious as the notes of a perfect organ . . .'

Young man: 'I . . .'

Tramp: 'Yes, yes. You went up to her, and poured out your heart . . . she noticed you were well dressed and she said yes. That's what happened, isn't it?'

Young man: 'You're so cruel. And yet, you're wrong. It is indeed a woman who's made me so happy, when she started to look on me favourably, but she's a woman who doesn't care about how people dress, or even how they look. All she demands is talent! Maybe she'd even smile at you, in spite of you having maligned her so much, just as she smiles at me. Her name is Gloria!'

Tramp: 'Ha, ha! I know that whore. You poor poet! Don't expect to enjoy her favours, she's too busy with the soldiers and politicians to even spare a thought for you. At the end of the day you're just a poor poet.'

Young man: 'You're a dangerous sceptic. But you won't poison me. I'm off.' (He stands up).

Tramp (staring at the young man and smoothing down bits of gravel in the sand, as if making a bed): 'Really?'

Young man: 'What are you doing?'

Tramp: 'I'm making a nice mattress for you, for when you come back here to lie down beside me.'

Young man: 'There's no point, I won't be back. Goodbye.' (He leaves).

Tramp (shaking his head and smiling): 'See you later!'

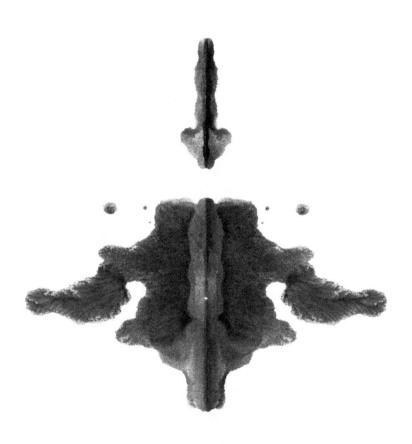

The First Burst of Laughter

When Gustavo announced the story of his romantic affair with a deadly serious face, we all started laughing.

'Romantic affair? You? Come on, you're kidding!'

But the expression on Gustavo's face became more and more serious. 'Yes, a romantic affair, yes; a stupid, precious, vulgar affair, with nocturnal sorties and sighs and laments and even suicide attempts, if you must know.'

'Impossible!' someone grunted. 'In order to be in love and to sing sweet laments at the feet of a lady of class you need to be serious for at least five minutes, and you're not capable of that.'

We all thought the same thing. Gustavo was a bit like a production line of good humour. When we were all gathered in the squalid little room that served as our abode, we could count out on our fingers how many days of fasting had gone by since our last scrap of supper; when problems as serious as the suspension of credit at the grocery store or an eviction for rent arrears were discussed, we had to insist by popular demand that he leave the room. It was impossible to talk about anything serious in the presence of such a happy soul who treated everything as a joke, even himself.

And now he came out with a story that he too was once in love, and had wept and taken things seriously, just like anyone else!

'And the worst thing is that by the look of it he's still in the grip of melancholy,' someone suggested.

'No, don't worry. The time has come to tell the story . . . the one about the Moorish Queen.'

Ah, yes. Our friend had often started to tell us that story. 'There was once a swarthy young maiden of fifteen summers . . .' Then the jokes would follow one after another and those of us waiting to hear the story would have make do with laughter. And now here we were again: we were starting to get interested. We waited a few moments and the man with the permanent sense of humour finally started to speak.

'She was a dark brunette, about fifteen years of age. Mischievous, playful and spiritual. Yes, spiritual too. I met her by chance. I came across her one day by the side of the road and her delicate little face, with her large dark eyes and her dainty red lips, seduced me. I approached her and we spoke.

She seemed to understand me and she accepted me immediately. She had discovered the dreamer in me, with my broad-brimmed hat, extravagant haircut and the look in my eyes, and she was a dreamer too.

As she told me in her adorable little voice, she dreamed about someone a bit like Lohengrin, about some enchanted prince from the ancient legends, who had come from a distant land, from the heavens, maybe, with armfuls of gold and myrrh in his soul, to deposit it all beneath the balcony of an enchanted queen, where the birds made their nests and an abundance of Andalusian carnations opened their sensuous mouths. She was the ideal woman, the Moorish Queen of all my dreams. To cut to the chase, it was a moment of happiness and that was all.'

'What happened next?'

'What happened next was what had to happen . . . I went away on a journey, one of my bohemian trips that took me to distant shores for a long time. When I came back, my Spanish balcony had been raided and the Moorish Queen with the large dark eyes and dainty red lips had been carried off. In her place was a woman having a conversation with another man. I was surplus to requirements there, maybe surplus to requirements in this world, and I wanted to die.

It was all settled in an instant. The prince wrote his final ballad, seized his dagger and headed towards the balcony where the birds made their nests and an abundance of Andalusian carnations opened their sensuous mouths. The rest of the story is self-evident. I woke up in time, I threw away the murderous dagger and instead of my final ballad, I hurled a first burst of laughter at the balcony.'

Juan Guerard's Supper

That day the brilliant idea of the crime had flashed through Juan Guerard's brain several times. At first it was like a feeling of burning hatred towards everything, like a strange desire to do something bad; then this feeling became more and more pronounced and as he was walking down a side street he noticed a little white cat in a doorway which was licking its whiskers calmly, so calmly it seemed to have forgotten that humans passed down there. Juan felt like giving it a good kicking. It was so pristine and chubby, so pretty and precious with a little bell dangling from a pink ribbon around its neck!

Juan had a vision of the bowl of food and saucer of milk provided to every spoilt cat and he was envious, he hated that contented little animal and the urge to splatter it was irresistible. As he passed close by, in spite of thinking that it was an act of brutality, he instinctively aimed a blow with the heel of his boot against the little animal's skull.

'Murderer! Heretic! Bandit! You'll rot in jail,' an old woman screeched at him from behind some latticework. 'Murderer!' Then he felt satisfied and he quickened his pace, smiling like a small boy proud of a piece of mischief.

Later, the memory of the little white cat splattered all over the pavement came into his thoughts in the form of a vague sense of remorse. He had always been so good and so sensitive, but when he thought about what he had just done he could barely recognise himself. Was he really turning into a bad person?

'Murderer! Bandit! You'll rot in jail,' he could hear the old woman screeching in his ear. 'Heretic! Bandit!' And he felt ashamed of himself and so repentant that he almost wanted to cry. But then, as he was walking along aimlessly and he saw a portly man with chubby cheeks coming towards him, exuding happiness through every pore of his skin, Juan thought that it was a pity he couldn't splatter a man's head as easily as the head of a cat.

* * *

It was now almost night time. The horizon was bloodied by the sunset and the twilight lent the surroundings a sinister red tinge that resonated in Juan's soul like an incitement to violence. Furthermore, the aroma of roast meat wafted into the street from people's kitchens, as if to remind passers-by that the residents of those houses were accustomed to having a decent meal.

And then Juan felt his hatred well up in his heart more than ever and he remembered that he hadn't eaten a morsel for twenty-four hours. He felt as if he had a wild beast inside him, biting at his soul and scratching at his stomach, like an impatient knight in armour digging his spurs into his mount to make it go faster. And then he realised that it was hatred he felt, more than hunger. And if at that moment he had come across a human heart and a plate of food, he wouldn't have hesitated to put the plate of food to one side in order to sink his teeth furiously into the human heart.

Just then he was walking across a square and, feeling exhausted, he collapsed on to a bench to reflect. Memories from the past flashed through his mind like a long caravan of visions, and he conversed at length with all his recollections.

First came his early childhood, innocently happy and rowdy, like a flock of white doves; then his adolescence, with his first hopes and first loves, subtle and fragrant as a garden in flower, like springtime. And after that happy train of thoughts had passed, he found himself back in his present life, as desolate and sterile as a nightmare in winter, littered with the debris of shattered dreams, broken hearts and disillusionment. Oh, people were so hateful and repugnant and vile!

He thought about his former office and his former life as a modest clerk. He remembered the hypocritical smiles and that hypocritical jealousy and all the baggage of hypocrisy that his colleagues carried on their shoulders, as they crawled on their knees from promotion to promotion and one degradation to the next. He remembered his superiors acting like sultans and the submissiveness of the eunuchs who aspired to their roles. Then he reconstructed the circumstances that had led to his dismissal. His boss's booming voice, roaring like a lion at his unconscionable audacity in responding haughtily to an unfair criticism; his colleagues' shock when they heard him shouting back at his boss; then his dismissal, trudging from firm to firm looking for a position; a frosty reception everywhere; hours waiting in corridors; every office manager saying 'come back tomorrow'; the first day without a meal; the first pangs of hunger; his inability to overcome it and his disgust at having to beg. And he felt proud of his current state. If he had been the same as everyone else, he would have felt ashamed, he would have found himself repulsive. But at least then he would have had something to eat.

* * *

'Oh Guerard, my dear Guerard!' Juan felt a pair of arms hugging him affectionately.

'What are you doing in these parts?'

It was Miguel Rodríguez, one of his former office colleagues, who had been promoted to his position when Juan had been dismissed.

'All of us in the office were so upset by your bad luck. The lads really liked you. What you did was totally mad, old chap. Bosses will be bosses: it's true they shout and sometimes insult you, but underneath it all they're not so bad. You have to put up with them, old chap, there's nothing else you can do.'

Juan felt put out by Rodríguez, but he contained himself. A

thought occurred to him, but then it made him feel so disgusted he had to spit. The idea had been to confess his situation and ask him for money for something to eat. Ah, hunger! Hunger!

'What are you doing now, old chap? Have you got a job? Are you all right?'

'I've got a job and I'm doing better than ever,' Juan replied proudly, as if wanting to rehabilitate himself in his own mind. 'I doubled my luck when I left that place.'

The other man did not reply, but after a moment's silence he spoke again.

'Come on, let's have something to drink, to toast your new situation.' And he dragged him by the arm to a local bar. Juan allowed himself to be led and accepted the invitation. They had a glass of cognac, then another round, then another and another.

Rodríguez was full of conversation and wittered on for over an hour about the office and his new position and his raise in salary and his duties and his bosses, anything that came into his head. Juan focussed back on himself and even forgot that there was someone else there who was talking to him. He leaned his elbows on the table and his chin on his fists, staring at the fourth glass of cognac, sitting in front of him, half empty.

The alcohol made him feel more gloomy. It hit his empty stomach like a hot coal and combined with his hunger to torture him even more. He almost could not cope any more with all his hatred. His companion had finally tired of talking. He looked at Juan, looked at his watch, called over the waiter and after paying the bill he went off, muttering to himself.

'The good for nothing has turned to drink. I always said that was how he'd end up.'

* * *

Juan watched his companion get up but he didn't stop him. He smiled stupidly and followed him to the door with a vague gaze, drained the remnants of his glass in one gulp and carefully took in his surroundings. The bar was full of locals, chatting and laughing noisily, while the degrading liquid flowed from bottles to glasses and from glasses to throats.

Then Juan thought again about people's stupidity, as he clenched his fists and the red mist clouded his mind again. He was a king, a strange king, covered in steaming, lukewarm blood which ran down his body like an embrace and bathed his feet and sprinkled his face and covered his hands like a glove. In front of him was a sumptuous table, covered in tasty morsels as strange and bloody as him. There was the body of the little white cat, the old woman's eyes sparkling with hatred and the happy passer-by's short fat neck. And he devoured all that bloody meat and savoured it delightfully, like an exquisite delicacy.

When he woke up, the café was almost deserted. At a table opposite him, two revellers were sharing a hearty supper and it was only then that Juan, seeing the food, felt human again. Hunger stirred inside him like a vampire sucking his blood until he was exhausted and he thought about death and felt faint. His neighbours at the opposite table, meanwhile, carried on chattering away happily. They were both young and they were both drunk. They were hardly eating anything, watching each other put away the drinks and splitting their sides with laughter. The plates of food remained in front of them almost untouched and the waiter was coming back and forth bringing fresh bowls of food or taking them away again.

Juan was staring like a fool at this with all his attention focussed on the plates of food. He felt weak, faint, humble and several times it occurred to him to beg them for the remnants of that banquet. Meanwhile the two young men carried on happily drinking, without noticing their ravenous neighbour. They drank more and more and laughed even more stupidly.

Suddenly, one of them began to sing and the other accompanied him in a long duet, tapping his glass with his fork. Then, apparently tired of this entertainment, he picked up a rib which was dripping blood on to his plate and threw it towards his companion's face. His companion ducked and the rib landed at Juan's feet like an invitation, and before he realised what he was doing, his teeth were tearing furiously at that scrap of bloody meat. The two drunkards watched in stupefaction, as if unable to comprehend.

'What a pig,' said one. The other one said, 'He's hungry.'
'Come over, my friend, we're all brothers here,' the first

man stammered. 'Come over.' And then, as if overcome with sentimentality, he added, 'Poor wretch. Who knows how long it's been since he last ate. You have to feel sorry for these wretches. Come over, brother, come over.'

Juan left his scrap of food on the table and looked at those men wide-eyed, without making a move and without saying a word.

Then, the first man who had spoken said, 'He's embarrassed.' And picking up a serving bowl full of food he staggered over to Juan, who watched him approach without moving and with his eyes wide open.

'Eat, brother, eat. Don't be embarrassed,' said the drunk, tottering in front of him with the bowl of food. 'Aren't you hungry? There's enough food here to fill you to bursting. Eat, man, eat.' And breaking off a bit of food, he lifted it towards Juan's mouth, wafting it first in front of his nose.

Juan made a movement as if to escape, then he felt his fists clench again, and the hunger wrench at his stomach and the blood cloud his vision. And he became a king again, and he turned his gaze back at the table covered in bloody morsels and he dreamed that he was devouring delightedly the short fat neck of the happy passer-by.

* * *

When he woke up, he found himself in the middle of a circle of men holding his arms and hitting him furiously.

66

Between his teeth was a piece of bloody meat, like the morsels on the strange king's table, and lying at his feet was the drunkard, with his throat mangled.

'Off to jail with him,' someone shouted. 'Lynch him, lynch him!' the others shouted furiously, and they all started pushing him and raining blows down on him. Then Juan remembered the little white cat and heard the old woman screeching and he let himself be led away, proud and smiling, like a small boy proud of a piece of mischief.

The Visionary

I liked him from the moment they told me he was mad. It was during one of my voyages. We'd left Genoa on the return journey to America. The steamship was enormous and there were a lot of passengers. In first class, there was a whole range of pot-bellied bourgeois gentlemen and idle youths who were travelling on business; in third class, it was pure pandemonium: hungry mouths, a horror show of ragged individuals who made a terrible racket, singing and laughing, dreaming of America, the promised land, where everyone was so happy and earned so much money and became so rich!

The steamship was loaded to the brim and low in the water under the weight of its enormous cargo of economic problems . . .

I might have been the only one who was travelling for the fun of it, the only one who was not in a rush to see the coastline of America. I laughed and was devilishly delighted when the sky turned black with clouds and the sea rose up like a mountain range, its peaks capped off with white foam.

He had come on board at Barcelona and by the time we arrived in Cadiz I had still not uncovered the mystery surrounding such a strange character.

No one knew who he was or what his name was or where he was heading. At first, it was rumoured that he was a Russian prince who was travelling incognito, then a Yankee millionaire . . . Eventually, everyone settled for the captain's version, and they all slapped their foreheads and said, 'I told you so!' as if to confirm their suspicions. The poor young man was a little bit touched, a monomaniac, a madman.

And when a rather precious spinster, making great efforts to look shocked, enquired whether his delusions mightn't be dangerous, and a solemn bourgeois gentleman with a large belly pointed out censoriously how inappropriate it was to have such a strange man on board, the captain smiled.

'He's a placid madman,' he said. 'His madness is emotional and tender. He's in love with a famous actress. The poor boy! If the doctors can't cure him, we'll end up with another poet. But there's no danger in that.'

And the respectable gentlemen and the elegant youths and spiritual young ladies welcomed the captain's words with a loud burst of laughter.

There was only one sigh and only one smile. The sigh came from the spinster who had asked about his delusions; the smile could be seen on my lips and was perhaps more clearly visible in my eyes. After that, no one brought up the subject again for serious discussion.

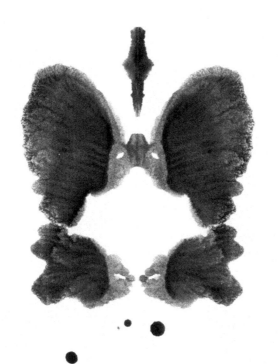

The Two Statues

His story was a vulgar story. He was born to a couple called Pérez or López or Rodríguez, into a comfortable bourgeois home, and he grew up surrounded by opulence, cossetted with care and affection and treats. When he left the seminary after an impeccable and thorough education he soon found himself in high society, where doors were unlocked by the 'open sesame' of his promise as a future millionaire, gaining him the admiration of all the men and the affection of all the women.

Set up as an idol by the magic endowed by gold coins and now the darling of the most refined society, he frequented all the salons, with the elegant affectations of a young playboy, driving the married women wild and their husbands to despair, a latter day Don Juan, until there was no more room in his address book which was filled with endless lists of the women he had betrayed and the men he had killed in duels.

His youth consisted of a long series of bold adventures. He outraged everyone time and time again, had umpteen brawls and so, making a mockery of women's imprudence and murdering innocent men, he led the vacuous life of an elegant bandit, always protected by his fame as a consummate swordsman and the wonderful magic of his gold coins.

When his parents died and he became the sole owner of a colossal fortune, he decided it was time to mend his ways. He left the orgies behind, withdrew from high society and spent the rest of his days devoted to his business, increasing his already fabulous wealth a hundredfold in bona fide bank deals, lending generously at ten per cent and cornering the market in commodities.

When he died, the whole of society, gathered together in the funeral chapel, discovered that the millionaire who had just passed away had been a philanthropist throughout his life. Before long, in the middle of the main square of the town where I live, a statue was erected on a granite plinth, an grandiose image of that saintly man 'who devoted his life to eradicating poverty and drying people's tears . . .' The whole town took part in an emotional procession past that statue, among them myself and my private tutor.

'Do you see?' said the old man, pointing at the monument that had just been unveiled. 'Watch, learn, and comprehend.'

* * *

The other man's story was no less vulgar, it is true. Doubtless conceived during an orgy in a brothel, he was probably born in a squalid attic room, maybe in a poorhouse, maybe in a prison . . . he never knew where or of whom. He spent his childhood wandering the streets and received his education in a prison, where he was taught all the criminal arts, perhaps by his very own father.

Then . . . the inevitable. Now well-schooled in his chosen

career, with a doctorate in crime, he made his living by marauding the high roads, robbing and killing and gracing the pages of the daily papers, filling their columns with the gory details of his barbarous deeds as an evil bandit.

One fine day, the police finally caught him. They brought him before the judges and he was condemned to the scaffold. One morning, a few weeks after the statue to the virtuous philanthropist was inaugurated, the body of the terrible evil-doer appeared opposite it, swinging from side to side, exhibited by the authorities as a public display of justice.

I remember it as clearly as if it had happened today. Hanging directly opposite the millionaire's statue, at the other end of the square, his fists clenched and his eyes almost jumping out of their sockets, he looked as if he was examining his neighbour with an expression of scorn, contempt, or rivalry. As we walked past him, my worthy tutor took me by the arm and pointed his finger at him.

'Watch, learn, and comprehend.'

* * *

These things happened many years ago. I left my home town and I have travelled far and wide. I have seen many statues and I have seen many hanged men and I have carried on watching and I have learned a lot, but I could never comprehend. And I am certain that I shall go to my grave unable to comprehend.

The Breakdown

What a fine couple! He was ugly, deformed, hunchbacked, but with a heart so big and generous that it more than made up for his body's deformity; she was beautiful, slim, provocative, but . . . exasperatingly simple-minded. How had fate conspired to unite those two people?

It was undoubtedly a sad act of madness on the part of them both. He saw her and was dazzled by her beauty, to the extent that, when he discovered her meanness of spirit it was already too late; love had found its way into his deformed chest and there was nothing that could be done about it.

She had just suffered a disappointment in love when she heard someone mention his work and describing him as a talented, turbulent poet, a cross between Orpheus and Quasimodo, immersed in the criminal underworld. She heard people speak about his devastating lines, hurled in the face of polite society like a flask of sulphuric acid, and she felt the perversely coquettish desire to snatch him from the crowd.

'We'll share his laurels,' she said to herself. 'From now on, he will write for me. I'll be the wife of one of the greatest poets, I'll be his muse. Oh, how my friends will envy me!'

And she offered the poet her lily-white hand. She had acquired a nightingale, just like any bourgeois lady who fills her patio with cages full of expensive songbirds, not to enjoy the sublime harmonies of their chirping, but to drive her neighbours mad with envy. Not to be dazzled but to dazzle others. So they were married and although they were happy for a short while, they soon realized that they had both made a mistake.

She never read his poems, except out loud when surrounded by her friends. She couldn't understand him! He became disillusioned and wounded, ever more unhappy as he fell deeper in love, and his poetry became ever more tender. Previously he had only known how to roar; now he wept! He realized that he had to make himself understood, and he completely forgot about the ordinary people, dedicating himself entirely to his beloved blonde princess. His usual muse, the muse of passionate emotions and intense feelings of hatred, was overcome by that beautiful, heartless bombshell. His devastating lines gave way to romantic madrigals.

But it was all in vain. Each day he became more convinced of the imminent disaster, each day her indifference became more pronounced and his love grew ever more intense.

He understood what was happening. He started off by reflecting on himself and ended up considering her position. Why should she love him if she couldn't understand him? And if she didn't love him, if she loved someone else, why should she stay with him, a slave to a love she didn't feel?

One day, after much struggling and much introspection, he had brought the subject up with her. 'You don't love me,' he told her. 'I suspect that you hate me, that you love someone else. That's fair enough. So why do you stay with me? I'm ugly, really ugly, almost deformed. You couldn't possibly love me. You are absolutely free, you have no obligation towards me, whereas you do owe a lot to yourself. You need to love someone, it's your duty, do you understand?'

But her only response was to weep and wail: 'You're so unfair. I do love you. Don't make me feel like a criminal.'

'A criminal? My poor darling!' he murmured, 'poor darling!' And he walked off, deeply worried. Was it true that she really did love him? And if she did not love him, was she so impoverished that she did not feel able to rebel?

* * *

That day he arrived home in a deep well of melancholy. He had reflected on so many things! Just as he was about to enter his study he stopped at the door and listened. Someone was in there, weeping. It was his wife.

He gently opened the door and stood there without moving for a few moments. It was her! Sitting at his desk with her back to the door, unaware of his presence, she carried on sobbing. She was clutching a sheet of pink notepaper: a love letter, beyond any doubt. Everything fell into place: a struggle between love and duty; those tears were born of a foolish stoicism.

Something stirred inside him, and it was decidedly not a fit of jealousy. He looked at her, first with pity and then with contempt. He hesitated for a moment, and then he went forward on tiptoes, until he was standing next to his sobbing wife.

She had a sheet of paper in front of her and she had started to scribble out a reply. 'Impossible.' Then her letter had been interrupted by grief: the word 'impossible' had been drenched with her tears.

'Poor darling!' he exclaimed, feeling a mixture of pity and disdain for that woman. 'Poor darling! She doesn't even have the courage to rebel!'

And without saying a word, without making a noise, he left the room, possessed of an infinite feeling of contempt towards that miserably impoverished soul who had closed her heart to her one true love, using the word 'impossible', bathed in tears, as a barrier.

The Quagmire

'Hey, young man, could you stop for a moment, please.' A corpulent gentleman with a large belly stood in my path. 'Is your name Herrera?'

'Yes, sir. And who are you?'

'I'm a policeman.'

'Oh, I see.'

'Would you do me the favour of accompanying me to the police station?'

'I'm very sorry, sir, but I don't do that kind of favour for anyone.'

'I'm afraid it's not optional.'

'Ah, well you should have said so in the first place. Let's go.'

And we started walking towards the police station, me with a sarcastic grin and the policeman looking increasingly concerned at seeing my grin. Then, as if unable to resist the doubts that were torturing him, he asked, 'Are you really Herrera?'

'Yes, of course I am. Were you worried you'd got the wrong man?'

'Oh no, not at all. When we arrest someone, we know exactly who they are.' Then he added, as if wanting to take me into his confidence, 'It's a thankless job, this, but what can you do? A man has to earn a crust, you understand . . .'

'Yes, of course. I understand only too well.'

'It's a job, like any other.'

'It's a little bit low.'

'Why do you say that?'

'Well, because you'll soon be replaced by something better. Haven't you heard of Belgian hounds? Apparently they do an excellent job as police officers.' And I grinned again.

The man with the large belly did not respond. Maybe he was annoyed at the intention behind what I had said, or maybe he was seriously reflecting on future competition. Wretched breeding kennels!

* * *

And here I am in prison. I am less of a brute and I am more well-meaning than most of the rabble; I love mankind and all I did was criticise the monarchy and the war. That makes me a seditionist.

The cell that they've put me in is not what I expected given the enormity of my crime. It is fairly spacious, there is ample light and I have a bed to sleep on, with a mattress and blankets and everything. Such generosity on the part of the police! The mattress is thick with parasites that will feast on me later with impunity. Marvellous! It is like going to an official reception at the palace.

* * *

Now it is the exercise period. The doors of all the cells have been opened with a deafening racket of squeaking hinges, spewing out their human contents into the prison yard. I am part of that enormous purge. Let us take a look at my companions. There are lots of them, lots and lots. Old, young and babes in arms; decrepit old men who are bent double like rotten trees, with no fruit and no sap and no flowers; adolescents full of energy and life, like green shoots sprouting from the earth, only to be buried in a quagmire. And they're all singing! And they're all laughing! Not a word of anger, not a sign of rebellion, not one melancholy smile. Peals of laughter and yet more peals of laughter.

Oh, mankind, mankind! All these objects in human form, do they not have souls? Possibly. But you could say that the poor devils are ashamed of looking themselves in the eye. Such is the world.

And when you think about it, all these stupid thieves could be just like grandees if fate had guided them on to the straight and narrow! And when you think about it, all these terrible murderers are nothing worse than peasant versions of military commanders! Oh, what glory could have been yours, you miserable wretches, if instead of being pickpockets you had been able to be bankers and instead of killing some random person you had spent your time killing Moors!

But, be patient. Justice is always depicted with a blindfold, her sword is equally sharp for everyone and her scales as true as any shopkeeper's. The law is the same for everyone!

*   *   *

The rabble parties on while I sit back and reflect. Then someone interrupts me.

'Hey, mate. You're new here, aren't you? Tell me straight. What did you do? Don't be embarrassed, don't be down. It's not so bad in here. At least you can be sure of a hunk of bread and some bean stew, not to mention the comfort of a bed that's almost as good as the ones in the Ritz.'

I offer him a cigarette, now we're like close friends. He'll be my guide in here.

'What do you want to know? What are this lot in here for? It's the same old things. Him over there stabbed a bloke, that one lifted someone's watch. Trust me, they're all good sorts.'

Suddenly, I notice a group of young men pass in front of us, fanning themselves and wiggling their hips as they go by, with a touch of feminine coquettishness. 'What about them?'

'Nancy boys. To hell with them. They bring shame on the prison. That one who looks a bit younger is "The Polar Star"; the one over there is "The Queen" and this one nearest us is "The Geisha Girl".' And my friend pointed to each of them in turn. They saw him and redoubled their efforts at posturing with a certain defiant arrogance. All of a sudden "The Queen", obviously guessing our comments, went over to the fountain and started washing some shirts, singing in an effeminate voice:

86

Me, I'm a working girl
And I take a pride in my trade

My friend shouted at him to 'Go to hell' and walked off. I stayed there, deep in thought. There is no question, even these types are important elements within our society. Given half a chance they would be princes or generals in Germany, or ministers of foreign affairs in Argentina. Poor androgenous creatures!

Recreation time was over, the prisoners were back in their cells and I was also returned to mine. When the door slammed shut, I fell on to the bed, no longer concerned about the bugs. 'Oh, what a society we live in!' I thought, and I recalled some paragraphs from a note sent to Prime Minister Maura by the Archbishop of Seville, regarding recent events: 'We must put an end for once and for all to these wretches who do nothing but sit around preaching antisocial ideas. We need to make an example of them.'

You are right, you big fat worm. We need to make an example of people who 'do nothing but sit around preaching antisocial ideas'. Let us see if we can finally achieve that.

Modelo Prison, Barcelona. July 1909.

The Two Sisters

'Why do you hate them so much, madam, those poor wretches?'

'#### #### ####!'

'Now then, don't get me going. They lead a revolting, disgusting life; their aims are unpleasant and base; their bodies weak and diseased. I know. They are cursed with every vice and affliction, we both agree on that. But you can't deny, madam, that all these syphilitics, with their moral and physical diseases, dressed up in all their finery in order to sell themselves in the local brothels, play an essential role in society. They are like latrines, where all human filth ends up. Their profession is almost like the priesthood, madam. All our Christian morals, which are absurd and unnatural, detract from life, so that love becomes a sin, and sins must be paid for, so love becomes a business activity. And furthermore, it's not their fault, madam. If God didn't send sinners to hell, then hell would have ceased to exist a long time ago.'

'#### #### ####?'

'What I mean is that it's not actually the foreigners or the ruffians or the old-fashioned *mesdames* that provide the brothels with fresh meat, that supply these immoral parties. It's our society's moral code; it's you, it's us. In short, it's decent people.'

'#### #### ####.'

'Evil minds, you say? Yes, I know. If those women, wanting to better themselves, had settled down to an honest job, they wouldn't be what they are today. It's true. In every city there are numerous factories relying on female labour. They work ten hours a day, sewing trousers, cleaning floors, packing cigarettes. Any woman can lead an honest life. All right. Is that all there is to it?'

'#### #### ####.'

'Listen, let me tell you a story. There were two sisters, one of them pretty, coquettish and promiscuous, like many who've gone before her. The other sister was ugly, shy and resigned, as docile as a sheep and as hard-working as an ant. But they were sisters.

They led a fairly comfortable life, but the day came when they realized that they had to take stock of their finances. The elder sister was nineteen years old, the younger one seventeen.

'What shall we do now?' they wondered.

'I'll get an honest job,' said the first one, 'and I'll earn enough to get by.'

The younger one said nothing. She pulled a face, shrugged her shoulders and one fine day she disappeared. She had a lover, then another one, then a lot more, and eventually she found herself down with the lowest of the low. She had a lover for a month . . . a lover for half an hour . . . what difference did it make? And she opted for the half-hour lover. She was a prostitute, like all the rest, exactly like all the rest. Ten years went by. The other sister, meanwhile, carried on working in her honest job . . . and she even won a prize for being virtuous.

So there you are, madam, two identical situations approached with two different mind sets. One opted for work and the other for vice. Both of them had their lives stolen from them, both of them sold themselves to put food on the table, but as you've seen, they followed completely opposite paths. And both of them died in a hospital, more or less at the same time, both of them burned out, both having struggled for a miserable crust of bread.'

'#### #### ####?'

'What difference was there between the two? I'll tell you, madam. One of them died in the Isolation Wing and the other in the ward for Venereal Diseases.'

My Friend's Mother

He looked sad and embittered and we became friends. There was so much melancholy behind those blue eyes! And in truth that boy became a really good soulmate. The day after we met we were already like brothers. We told each other about our past lives and confided our hopes and plans.

He was all alone in the world and he was something of a misanthropist; he lived in a small white, delightfully poetic house in the suburbs, as quiet as an elf in the depths of a garden. His father had died young, worn out by life as an inveterate playboy. He was an only child and he inherited a modest annuity.

As for his mother . . . he had never known anything about his mother. A purely physical love affair; a quick fling; a woman abandoned a few months after giving birth: that had been his origin. His father, a few hours before he died, had told him about it.

'Try to find her. The poor thing was a really good woman and I treated her abominably. Forgive me.'

And he kissed his father on the forehead, unaware then of what his father was telling him, and told him that there was nothing to forgive. He had been just a young lad at the time!

'Oh, if only I could find her!' my poor friend would sob. And it became something of an obsession for him.

'It must be so wonderful to have a mother!' he would say,

and his eyes would light up and he would start to outline a series of ingenious plans. He would bring her home to live with him, in his little white house in the suburbs, and the pair of them would be so happy together!

But the years went by and his mother did not appear. Maybe she had got married, maybe she had died . . . And once again those blue eyes, so full of melancholy, were clouded over with sadness.

'What you need is a woman to love you, Alfredo. Why don't you get married?'

'Married! You're right.' He'd never thought about marriage. But first he needed to find his mother.

'She must be around forty, by now,' he added. 'When my father met her she was still very young. The poor little thing must have suffered so much! But one day I'll find her, don't you think?' And his eyes would gleam again with pleasure.

'Yes, I'm sure you'll find her. You'll bump into her the day you least expect it. You'll see, my dear friend, you'll see.'

Then he'd look at me as if he were grateful, full of childish joy.

'Oh! How happy that would make me!'

* * *

Unusually, very late last night, my friend appeared in my room. He was pale and distraught, in his shirt sleeves, panting strangely, like a madman. He came in without saying a word

94

and flung himself down on my bed, burying his head in the pillow, weeping desperately.

'I found her, I found her.'

I suspected a personal tragedy and tried to calm him down.

'Don't be a baby. Tell me what happened and let's see if we can find a solution. For goodness sake! What's happened to your resilience, my dear friend?'

After a long while he calmed down and told me what had just happened. He'd had a late supper. He was feeling depressed and he'd had a lot to drink, far too much. And then he felt like his head was weighing him down and he needed a breath of fresh air, so he went out into the street to take a stroll. He carried on walking for quite some time, wandering nowhere in particular, completely at random, when he suddenly found himself in the middle of a red light district.

'How revolting it was!' Smelly taverns full of women, thugs and soldiers, all of them drunk, and they were singing and drinking in the thick of that atmosphere of vice and decay, using foul language and obscene gestures, with a nauseating lasciviousness. He had felt a deep repugnance at the whole scene. The alcohol worked on his brain in a strange way, heightening details, increasing the intensity of all the unpleasant sensations. He wanted to get out of there as soon as possible and he started walking faster. He began to run. Suddenly he heard someone calling out to him and he stopped. He was right in front of a brothel, by a window.

'Come on in, sweetheart, come inside.' A woman was

leaning out of the window. He looked at her. She was not young or beautiful, but there was something about that prostitute's face, like the vestiges of an expression of purity that vice had not quite managed to destroy. He felt mysteriously attracted. He went in and enjoyed the woman's caresses.

'I realised that she was staring at me, really staring, so I asked her, 'why are you looking at me like that?'

'You remind me of my first lover,' she said. 'He was like you, with fair hair and blue eyes.'

We were silent for a while and she carried on looking at me.

'How old are you,' she asked. Then I began to feel uncomfortable. I should have told her where to go, but I couldn't. 'Twenty-two,' I replied sharply, and I began to put on my clothes.

'Twenty-two. Twenty-two years old!' she murmured. And after hesitating for a long while, she decided to interrogate me again, half-curious and half-fearful.

'Tell me, what is your name?'

'What's my name? Why do you want to know? My name is Alfredo Méndez. Why?'

Her eyes opened wide and she asked me a question which really enraged me.

'Your mother . . . did you know her?'

My indignation exhausted what was left of my patience. The miserable wretch! That miserable prostitute, that filthy whore, had just profaned the memory of my mother, in a brothel! Rage and alcohol did the rest. I threw myself on that woman and slapped and punched her in a rage. It was all over in a flash. She didn't try to defend herself. I felt disarmed and realized what a terrible thing I'd done. I apologised, I begged her forgiveness. She didn't reply, but she looked at me tenderly and after a moment she questioned me again.

'And your father . . . tell me, did your father have the same name as you?'

I felt as if the world was crashing down around me.

'Yes, my father had the same name as me. Why do you ask, tell me, why do you ask?' And I began to shake her violently. 'Tell me, spit it out, why do you ask?'

She was frozen in horror. She looked at me wide-eyed, unable to speak a word. Then she covered her face with the sheet and began to weep inconsolably.

'The horror! The horror!'

I stayed there, frozen to the spot like an idiot, without managing to move an inch, without managing to say a word.

Then, seized by a sudden fit of madness, I tore the sheet from her face and started to shake her again, crushing her against the bed, roaring in despair, 'No, you wretch, no. You're not her! You're not her!'

* * *

That was all my friend said. He pressed his face into the

97

pillow again and started to sob once more. I did not even try to console him. What was the point?

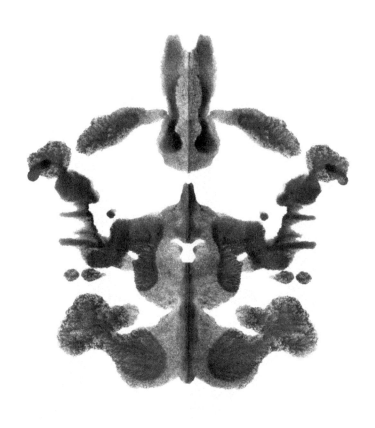

Suggestion

'Yes, there's no getting away from it,' the miserable country boy murmured through gritted teeth, 'Concepción the Black Woman is wrong. Trinidad loves me, she told me so. She swore to me as she was fighting back her tears on the day she went away. Anyway . . .' he added, as if swept by a new wave of bitter scepticism, 'Anyway, like my grandfather used to say, if a woman's tears . . .'

And the arguments for and against swirled around in his heated imagination, as a long train of memories trundled slowly past.

'It can't be true, it can't be true, Concepción the Black Woman is wrong.' And straight away the screeching voice of the black *Mama God* began to ring in his ears, always ready to squawk out his disappointments, always ready to sneer at his adolescent naivety.

But the black woman couldn't be wrong. She knew how to call up the spirits and divine people's destinies and read the irrevocable sentences of fate in the lines on the palms of their hands. She had predicted the demise of Don Pancho, the ranch owner from La Palmera who had died exactly two months later, murdered at the crossroads, as he left Meneguina the Gringo's saloon. She knew when there was going to be a drought and when the locusts were coming and when war was about to break out. She had cured the little

Indian boy, the son of the resident of 'the two paths', who would later be killed by parasites. She had cured the stallholder at Los Talos from a magic spell, and she knew how to make that marvellous ointment that could heal wounds and cure the evil eye.

No, *Mama God* the Black Woman couldn't be wrong. But could it be that Trinidad—the young girl who had grown up together with him, who had run through the fields with him and had gone with him to their first parties and had tasted her first kisses with him as a woman—had forgotten about him? And why couldn't Concepción the Black Woman be wrong?

And then he was swamped by memories and he felt himself flushed with the ineffable sweetness of a first romance. They had grown up together and said that they loved each other ever since they could first understand what that meant. They had played at being lovers like grown-ups ever since they were small children, and when they were grown-ups they had still felt tenderly innocent, like children. They had loved one another so much, they had been so happy all that time! And later . . . The poor man's forehead creased at the thought of 'later'.

One day, her father had taken ill and decided to give up working in the fields, rent out the ranch and retire to a quiet life in the town. He was old and the girl was now a young woman and, what the devil! He was wealthy and he should be thinking about her education, making her mix with other people; after all, she wasn't going to spend her whole life living in the countryside like an animal . . .

And so they were separated, after many tears and many kisses, many tears and many promises, and in their absence they had carried on loving one another the same as before. He adored her just as much and she loved him even more, she swore she did in her letters, those letters couched in tender words in which he saw her soul reflected, just as in days gone by he had seen her pretty face reflected in the clear water of the stream. He was obsessed with her. Through the hours of hard toil and danger and disappointment, through anything and everything, he was comforted by the marvellous balm of those words, 'I will love you always', unfailingly delivered in those tender messages, those poorly scrawled sheets of white paper, on which he could always detect her still fresh tear stains.

Now, for more than a month, alarmingly, the letters had stopped coming. For a month now the stagecoach had driven past each day without stopping by the gate, without bringing him anything except the tedious sarcastic comments of the wretched foreman.

What had happened to his Trinidad? Had she left the town? Maybe she was ill? And although he turned it over in his mind a thousand times, trying to find the reason for such an anomaly, the thought had never occurred to him that his darling Trinidad might have forgotten him.

That day, the stagecoach had appeared in the distance and had slowly made its approach like a burgeoning hope; then as it passed by without stopping and raced away, disappearing into the dust clouds as if all hope were vanishing, the poor man thought he was dying.

A riot of ideas rattled around in his head and in his heart he felt a whole conspiracy of fateful omens; mad with despair and barely aware of what he was doing, he jumped on his horse and galloped six leagues and finally came to a halt, almost without knowing how, at the house of Concepción the Black Woman, the most revered clairvoyant in the whole district of Las Chircas.

* * *

He left there with his head burning and his heart in pieces. The black witch doctor, after a thousand theatrical turns and a thousand pantomime stunts, had evoked all the spirits in the district, and resolved to speak plainly, telling him more or less:

'Listen, country boy, don't get upset, even the best gaucho can be trashed by a coward, and the craftiest man can be fooled by a fox. The girl's deceiving you, she's forgotten all about you, but that's not the worst of it, because something even little children know is that a woman's heart is falser than a cave full of Turkish trinkets. The worst of it is what I can read in the future. There's something there that's telling me that at midnight, when the witches come out of their hiding places and the tormented souls are out and about, flying

104

through the air, the besotted country boy, unable to withstand the blow that fate has dealt him, is going to ask this old soothsayer to take him for a ride to the cemetery.'

* * *

And there he was, rooted in his chair, desperately churning through all his memories, in front of the pine desk where an ancient pistol—the type that you loaded down the barrel—had languished undisturbed for the past two decades. His grandfather, in whose hands the weapon had served in the days of his youth, used to say that it had a pact with death and had been the decisive factor in numerous incredible situations of doubtful authenticity, but now it was an almost useless contraption.

And superstition weighed down on his mind, while the arguments for and against swirled around in his head, and he made a final effort to grapple with that fatal obsession, like an entranced bird flying its last circuits around the mouth of a snake.

The shrill shriek of an owl shook him out of his reverie; the broken clock that he had also inherited from his grandfather struck twelve. That was fatal. Concepción the Black Woman could never be wrong. It had to happen.

As if taken over by a supernatural force, he clasped his hand around the pistol, brought it slowly up to his temple, squeezed the trigger and waited for death like a hero.

But death did not come. The pistol must have been unloaded.

For a long time the country boy waited there in suspense, his hand clenched around the old pistol. Then he brought it down slowly, inspected it for a moment, half mocking and half disappointed, and flung it contemptuously on to the old bunk, more convinced than ever of his darling Trinidad's love.

ALSO AVAILABLE FROM THE CLAPTON PRESS

THE YOCCI WELL by Juana Manuela Gorriti
A love story, ghost story and gothic horror rolled into one, the action of this brilliant novella spans 25 years, encompassing the Argentine War of Independence and the brutal civil wars that followed. Published now for the first time in English.

OUR NATIVE LAND by Juana Manuela Gorriti
This is the first published translation into English of *La tierra natal*, Juana Manuela Gorriti's last major work, which relates a physical journey through northern Argentina as well as a voyage back through her memories of the people and events she had known and experienced along the way.

MY HOUSE IN MALAGA by Sir Peter Chalmers Mitchell
While most ex-pats fled to Gibraltar in 1936, Sir Peter stayed on to protect his house and servants from the rebels. He ended up in prison for sheltering Arthur Koestler from Franco's rabid head of propaganda, who had threatened to 'shoot him like a dog'.

**BRITISH WOMEN AND THE SPANISH CIVIL WAR
by Angela Jackson – 2020 Edition**
Angela Jackson's classic examination of the interaction between British women and the war in Spain, through their own oral and written narratives. Revised and updated for this new edition.

BOADILLA by Esmond Romilly
The nephew that Winston Churchill disowned describes his experiences fighting with the International Brigade to defend the Spanish Republic. Written on his honeymoon in France after he eloped with Jessica Mitford.

SOME STILL LIVE by F.G. Tinker Jr.
Frank Tinker was a US pilot who signed up with the Republican forces because he didn't like Mussolini. He was also attracted by the prospect of adventure and a generous pay cheque. This is an account of his experiences in Spain.

ALSO AVAILABLE FROM THE CLAPTON PRESS

NEVER MORE ALIVE: INSIDE THE SPANISH REPUBLIC
by Kate Mangan, with a Preface by Paul Preston
When her lover, Jan Kurzke, made his way to Spain to join the International Brigade in 1936, Kate Mangan went after him. She ended up working with Constancia de la Mora in the Republic's Press Office, where she met a host of characters including WH Auden, Stephen Spender, Ernest Hemingway, Robert Capa, Gerda Taro, Walter Reuter and many more. When Jan was seriously injured she visited him in hospital, helped him across the border to France and left him with friends in Paris so she could return to her job in Valencia.

THE GOOD COMRADE, MEMOIRS OF AN INTERNATIONAL BRIGADER
by Jan Kurzke, with an Introduction by Richard Baxell
Jan Kurzke was a left-wing artist who fled Nazi Germany in the early 1930s and tramped round the south of Spain, witnessing first-hand the poverty of the rural population, later moving to England where he met Kate Mangan. When the Spanish civil war broke out in 1936, Jan went back and joined the International Brigade, while Kate followed shortly after, working for the Republican press office. Many of his fellow volunteers died in the savage battles on the outskirts of Madrid and Jan himself was seriously wounded at Boadilla, nearly losing his leg. This is his memoir, a companion volume to *Never More Alive.*

IN PLACE OF SPLENDOUR: THE AUTOBIOGRAPHY OF A SPANISH WOMAN
by Constancia de la Mora, with a foreword by Soledad Fox Maura
Constancia de la Mora was the grand-daughter of Antonio Maura, who had served under Alfonso XIII as Prime Minister. She was one of the first women to obtain a divorce under the fledgling Spanish Republic. During the civil war she became a key figure in the Republic's International Press Office, moving to the USA and Mexico after the war was lost. This is her remarkable memoir, with a detailed history of the build-up to the conflict.

ALSO AVAILABLE FROM THE CLAPTON PRESS

SPANISH PORTRAIT by Elizabeth Lake
A brutally honest, semi-autobiographical novel set in San Sebastián and Madrid between 1934 and 1936, portraying a frantic love affair against a background of confusion and apprehension as Spain drifted inexorably towards civil war.

MARGUERITE REILLY by Elizabeth Lake
First published in 1946, Marguerite Reilly is the fictionalised story of four generations of Irish immigrants struggling to make good in the Victorian and post-Victorian era, from the days of the Great Hunger up to the end of the second world war. Harrowing at times but always entertaining, this is a must-read for anyone with Anglo-Irish heritage.

FIRING A SHOT FOR FREEDOM: THE MEMOIRS OF FRIDA STEWART with a Foreword and Afterword by Angela Jackson
Frida Stewart drove an ambulance to Murcia to help the Spanish Republic and visited the front in Madrid. During the Second World War she was arrested by the Gestapo in Paris and escaped from her internment camp with help from the French Resistance, returning to London where she worked with General de Gaulle. This is her previously unpublished memoir.

STRUGGLE FOR THE SPANISH SOUL & SPAIN IN THE POST-WAR WORLD by Arturo and Ilsa Barea, with Introduction by William Chislett.
During the Spanish Civil War, Arturo and Ilsa Barea worked for the Republic's Press and Censorship office, operating from the Telefónica building in Madrid. They later sought refuge in the UK, where Arturo broadcast weekly bulletins to Latin America for the BBC World Service. *Struggle for the Spanish Soul*, an essay on contemporary Spain calling on the democracies of Europe to unseat Franco, was published in 1941. Spain in the post-war world, published in 1945, made similar arguments, which also fell on deaf ears. Together the two essays present a horrific picture of the early years of the dictatorship, which was to endure until Franco's death in 1975.

111

ALSO AVAILABLE FROM THE CLAPTON PRESS

THE FIGHTER FELL IN LOVE: A SPANISH CIVIL WAR MEMOIR by James R Jump, with a Foreword by Paul Preston and a Preface by Jack Jones
Aged twenty-one, James R Jump left his Spanish fiancée in England and went to Spain to join the International Brigade. He was mentioned in despatches for bravery during the Battle of the Ebro. His previously unpublished memoir brings back to life his time in Spain and the tragic course of the war he took part in, while the accompanying poems reflect the intense emotions sparked by his experience.

SINGLE TO SPAIN & ESCAPE FROM DISASTER by Keith Scott Watson
The author joined the International Brigades in Spain to defend the Republic against Franco's fascist rebellion. He saw action at Cerro de los Ángeles alongside Esmond Romilly and resigned shortly afterwards, staying on in Madrid as a war correspondent. Within a few weeks, most of the British volunteers in his battalion were dead and he had been chased out of Spain as a deserter. *Single to Spain* is his memoir of those experiences, first published in 1937. He soon returned to Spain and was one of the first journalists on the spot to report on the bombing of Guernica in April 1937. *Escape from Disaster* is his report on the fall of Barcelona and his desperate dash for the border in January 1939, first published in 1940.

www.theclaptonpress.com